TRICK OR TRENT

DOGG PACK SERIES
BOOK 5

EVIE MITCHELL

THUNDER THIGHS PUBLISHING

ACKNOWLEDGEMENT OF COUNTRY

I acknowledge the Traditional Custodians of the lands on which I write, the Ngunnawal people, and pay my respect to elders both past and present.

I acknowledge the continued and deep spiritual relationship of the Australian Aboriginal and Torres Strait Islander peoples' to this land, and their unique cultural and spiritual relationships to the land, waters and seas and their rich contribution to society.

Always was, always will be.

To my Greedy Readers.
Thank you for waiting for this book.
I hope you know that you are loved just as you are.

And as always—to my husband.
Thank you for choosing me every day.

TRICK OR TRENT

Ryan

I don't look like your typical arson investigator. But I happen to have a knack for solving fires... Pity I'm a failure when it comes to subduing my own burning desires...

After ten years one would assume the flame I carried for my high school sweetheart would well and truly be extinguished. Not so, it seems.

Trent's returned home, and it appears the sparks are flying in more ways than one.

Trent

I knew returning to Capricorn Cove after nearly ten years wouldn't be a walk in the park. But I didn't expect to be navigating crime scenes with my ex-boyfriend.

Why does Ryan have to look so gorgeous?

Why does he have to be so kissable? And since when did he learn to do *that* with his tongue???

He better be careful, cause I'm about to burn all his walls down.

Warning: This book is complete fluffy nonsense with two men who adore each other, fire, Halloween, and a touch of small-town madness. Welcome to the Dogg Pack!

CHAPTER 1

Ryan

"**S**hit, shit, shiiiiiiiiiitttttttttt!" My sister-in-law's scream echoed through the parking lot from the backseat of the car in which she was sprawled.

Sprawled and currently in labour.

Shit.

Beyond the cars and trees, the gravel lot remained empty of living creatures but for a few crows pecking innocently at the ground.

Shit, shit shit!

"Just breathe, Hazel. In and out, in and out." I made a huffing sound, trying to act as if I knew what the fuck to do in this situation.

Spoiler alert: I did not.

"Where's the ambulance?" she panted, her face red and blotchy.

That is a damned good question.

"On its way," I promised.

"And James?"

"Also, on his way."

I fucking hope.

Hazel turned her tear-glistening gaze on me. "What am I going to do, Ryan? I can't have this baby here. James hasn't missed one birth. He can't miss this one."

After three kids, you'd think he'd know better.

I looked around the parking lot of the restaurant, Pier Pressure, and silently cursed her craving for burgers.

I should never have listened to her. I should never have given in to a pregnant woman's pleas. Just one burger, she said. It'll be fine, she said. The woman is a week overdue and now look at us. Stranded in a carpark with no help and no way of transporting her safely.

I better be named Godfather for this.

"Look, babies take forever, right?" I lied, having no idea despite being the uncle to numerous kidlets. "Don't worry too much. The ambulance will be here any—"

I broke off as Hazel nearly crushed the bones in my hand, her body bowing as she groaned through another contraction.

Despite the overwhelming pain in my hand, I managed to peek at my watch.

Fuck. That's two minutes. Fuck!

I glanced out the car window, desperately searching for someone—anyone—to help me.

"Hey! You! Help!"

The guy turned, the sun at his back blocking me from seeing him clearly.

"Me?" he asked.

"Yeah, I need towels and hot water and—" I stuttered, at a loss for what else I might need. "Can you just... help? My sister's having a baby."

"Shit! I'm on it."

The guy sprinted off as I turned back to Hazel, finding her gripping her knees, her body curved up.

"Ryan—I think she's—"

"Fuck!" I bent and gripped the edge of her skirt. "You okay if I have a lo—"

"Just do it!"

Alright then.

I flicked up her skirts and nearly passed out at the sight of a head coming out of her vagina.

Dear gods above. Women choose to do this?

Fuck, I'm gonna be sick.

No, you got this, Ryan. You have to have this.

Hold it together, dude!

HOLD IT TOGETHER!

Hazel let out a long, low groan, straining as I got into position, ready to catch the baby.

Distantly I heard a car skidding to a halt behind me as Hazel panted through another long contraction.

This will be fine. All will be fine. Everything is fine. Everything is—

"Hazel!"

I sagged in relief at my brother's familiar bellow.

"Oh, thank god." I shifted from my kneeling position. "Hurry, James!"

My brother elbowed me out of the way, arriving in time to catch his daughter as she slid silently into the world.

For a second, my heart caught, fear striking deep when she didn't stir.

"Shit! Is she—?"

Just as I was about to ask if she was okay, the baby began to squirm, her little limbs moving as she sucked in her first, deep breath. Her red face screwed up, her tiny rosebud mouth opening to let out an almighty angry scream.

"Oh! Wow!" A hand pressed to my back. "Here are your towels."

Linen was pressed into my arms, and I automatically moved close to where James was placing the baby on Hazel's chest. I wrapped them in the clean beach towels, mindful of the umbilical cord.

The baby's eyes blinked open, her limbs settling as the colourful fabric wrapped around her, swaddling her tight.

I stared into her stunning blue eyes, my heart falling at her tiny feet.

"Hey there, little Bubba," I cooed, the sounds of emergency sirens beginning to wail in the background. "I'm your Uncle Ryan. You're gonna be an absolute firecracker, aren't you? Arriving so quickly."

Her wailing kicked up a notch, her precious face red and flushed. My heart jolted and a rush of protective love flooded over me.

"Such anger! Don't worry, babe. I'll help you slay all your dragons."

I looked up, finding Hazel watching me, tears in her eyes.

"You okay, Mumma?"

She nodded and I stepped back, watching as the family began to bond even as the paramedics swarmed the scene.

"Excuse me, could you move, please? We need to create a bit of space here." One of the paramedics waved me back.

Where were you five minutes ago, dude?

"Great catch, Ryan."

The man's voice registered, the tone and the

timbre achingly familiar. I turned, coming face-to-face with the man who'd broken my heart nearly ten years ago.

I froze, my entire body turning to ice. "T-Trent?"

He held out one of the towels. "You have some blood on your arms."

I looked down, absently noting the red lines. "Oh, right. Thanks."

I absently cleaned myself as I stared at him, registering all the things I'd missed when I'd first spoken to him in my panic.

Oh, dear.

He wore damp board shorts, running shoes and nothing else. Water droplets fell from his curly hair down across his infinitely kissable umber skin, making his chest sparkle in the late afternoon sun. He'd always had an athletic build, but the six-pack he now rocked was new —and intimidating.

Trent had always been attractive, but now he looked like some kind of superhero, all bronze and gorgeous with a hint of helpful mischief while I sat in stark contrast with my pasty-white, almost sickly, complexion and slight stomach pudge.

Time to lay off Karen's cooking.

My mouth went dry as Trent reached up to

brush a stray droplet from his forehead, his bicep and abdomen flexing with the movement.

Why does he look so good? This is fucking torture.

He doesn't. He's the embodiment of the devil, remember?

Objectively, he does. I can't deny it.

Yes, I can. He looks like he'll break your heart.

Trent tilted his head to one side. "You look good, Ryan."

And you look like the ex-I-never-want-to-see-again.

I forced a gritted-teeth smile.

"Thanks," I muttered, aware that he'd caught me in what had to possibly be the third worst way to reconnect with an ex. "What are you doing in town? Visiting your sister?"

"I've moved back."

My gaze whipped up to meet his. "Excuse me? As in... to the Cove?"

"Yeah." He watched me process this news.

Danger Will Robinson, danger!

"I... well," I cleared my throat. "Welcome back, I guess."

I guess???? Could I be any more obvious?

Fuck. I better start shopping for one-way tickets to Australia. Are they sending people to the moon yet? What about Mars? Surely a megalomaniac billionaire is interested in Human trials for space expeditions.

Trent tilted his head to one side, a small grin playing on his lips. "Looks like we'll be seeing a lot of each other from now on."

"I don't know about that. Capricorn Cove has grown since you last lived here," I said, desperately denying his statement.

"Ryan! We need you."

I turned to walk away, calling over my shoulder. "Bye, Trent."

"See you soon, Ryan."

I nearly spluttered.

Over my dead body.

CHAPTER 2

Trent

Ryan practically sprinted across the carpark to where the woman and newborn were being loaded onto an ambulance. I watched him laugh and joke with her as the paramedic lifted the bed onto the truck.

He looked good.

No, he looked better than good. He looked good enough to lick from head to toe.

Some things never change.

I rubbed a hand over my tight chest.

And some things do.

I'd left the Cove nearly a decade ago, determined to explore everything the world had to offer. I'd hated our small town—with its nosy neighbours and lack of opportunities. I'd seen it as a cage, its bars growing ever closer every second I remained here.

Ryan hadn't seen it that way. After a childhood spent in and out of foster homes, he'd been content to remain here, happy to trade gossip and generate it. Happy to be close to family and friends.

I was the wind to his tree. Where he wanted deep roots, I needed to be free to chase wide-open horizons.

Our differences were what had made us work—and what ultimately led to our demise.

"Tee, you ready?"

I turned to my sister, grinning as she bounced her way across the gravel park toward me, her wet swimsuit leaving a water trail behind her.

"Yeah."

Faye frowned as she caught sight of the ambulance. "Did someone have an accident?"

It was a fair question. The woods surrounding Lover's Lake were part of the Capricorn Cove National Park—a popular hiking and camping area throughout the year. While the local park service made all efforts to keep the trails clear and as safe as possible, accidents tended to happen.

"Not quite." I slung an arm over her shoulder, guiding her along to my car. "A baby decided this is where they wanted to be born."

"Wow. I hope they're okay."

"They seemed to be, last I saw."

Faye flicked her towel over her shoulder and glanced up at me, her dark eyebrow arching in question. "You saw them?"

"I might have had to sacrifice our spare towels to assist with the birth."

"Ha! That's awesome. Who was it?"

"I'm not sure, but it looked like Hazel Dogg. Ryan was there and—"

Faye stopped short, and I stumbled beside her at her sudden stillness.

She twisted, staring at me with big eyes. "You saw Ryan?"

I inwardly sighed, knowing what was about to come.

"Yeah."

"And?" she asked, her foot beginning to tap out a beat on the gravel, sending tiny puffs of dust into the autumn air.

"And?" I repeated, crossing my arms over my chest.

She sighed dramatically, her dark eyes flashing as she threw her arms up. "How did it go?"

"Fine." I shrugged. "It's not like we stopped to chat, Faye. He'd just helped deliver a baby."

My sister glared at me with an expression I was all too familiar with.

Hell is about to reign upon me.

Short and slim with a lovely smile, my sister radiated sunshine and happiness. One would never suspect the temper contained within her small frame.

Napoleon syndrome, my mother had once said with an exasperated sigh. From a young age, Faye had been the tiny dictator in our lives, determined to get what she wanted through persuasion or domination.

With a dramatic sigh, Faye shook her head as if done with me.

"What?" I asked defensively.

"You'll find out," she warned, brushing past me on her way to the car. "And if you don't, then it's your loss."

Rolling my eyes, I trailed behind her.

I'd been away a long time, and driving back to town reminded me of all the things I'd unknowingly missed when I'd been away.

Outside the car windows, the world was on fire, each leaf painted with the colours of autumn. Gold and red foliage ruffled in the semi-warm breeze—no doubt a last hurrah before the cool weather began to descend. Already the smell of nutmeg, ginger and cinnamon seemed to vibrate in the air, while pumpkins and ghosts decorated doorsteps along with apple-mangers.

"Why do we have apple mangers?" I asked Faye as we drove passed yet another yard stacked with an overflowing apple cart.

"It goes back to the First Peoples," she answered absently as she flicked through her phone. "The Manari have a tradition that during the autumn harvest, they share their bounty with those who are less fortunate. Traditionally, the carts or mangers would have all sorts of abundant produce in it. But at some point, as the tradition continued, people stopped offering different types of produce and now only do apples."

"Interesting." I hit the indicator and turned left down her street. "Your house is standing in stark contrast to the one next to it."

She chuckled. "That's Honey Rodriguez. Do you know her husband, Tristan?"

I tried to place the name. "Sheriff, right?"

"Mmhmm. She owns the physical therapy clinic in town."

I pulled into her driveway. "Let me guess. It's the shop with the crazy Halloween display?"

Faye laughed. "Got it in one."

I waved at Faye's roommate who stood spraying a hose across their brownish patchy lawn. "I'm not sure that's going to help."

"Hope lives in hope."

"Hope would do better to leave the grass alone."

Faye chuckled. "For someone who grew up on a farm, she definitely lucked out of the green thumb." She leaned across the centre console to press a kiss to my cheek. "Good luck tomorrow."

I blew out a breath. "Thanks."

"Say hi to the parentals for me."

I nodded, flexing my hands on the steering wheel.

As much as I loved my parents, I was too old and far too independent to be under their roof for longer than a few weeks.

She slid from the car then leaned down, her smile wide. "By the way, the house at the end of the street on the left?" She pointed down the way. "That's Ryan's."

With that piece of gossip, she shut the door and skipped toward her porch. I poked my head out the car window.

"Foul play!"

She laughed, flipping a dismissive hand over her shoulder as she disappeared inside.

Curiosity shouldn't have been biting at my heels with this new information. Our relationship ended our final year of high school. Ryan had been accepted into a local university, while I'd been offered a scholarship in Australia.

It had been an emotionally rough time for both of us as we'd stripped back the layers of who we were as a couple to realise that we were incompatible individuals.

Ryan hadn't taken it well. And, truth be told, neither had I. My final months of high school had been fraught with a series of manoeuvres I'd deemed necessary to avoid the boy I'd loved.

I tapped my hand on the steering wheel watching Hope turn what little grass covered their front lawn into a wet mud pile.

"Fuck it," I muttered, putting the car in reverse. "One drive-by won't kill me."

I inched down the road, taking in the mix of new and old builds. Capricorn Cove had undergone a transformation over the last decade as new families moved in and began to gentrify the small town.

All the things I'd once hated had somehow become the things I'd most missed. The slow pace of the town. The familiar sweeping landscape and the way it differed depending on the weather. Hell, I'd even missed being the subject of the occasional gossip circle.

For a man who'd spent the better part of a decade running from my past, it felt strange to have reconciled.

Nothing had prompted my return to the Cove. No life-changing moment or ill relative.

When the job listing had popped up, I'd made the decision. It had just felt right.

My car slowed to a crawl as I drew even with Ryan's house, taking in the small beach bungalow with its neat garden hedges and pleasant flower beds.

Everything about it screamed domestic bliss—and strangely, I found myself liking it.

A man opened the door of the house as I slowly rolled by. He stepped out onto the porch. He wore grey sweatpants and no shirt as he stretched, rubbing a hand over his face.

He was young, attractive, and shockingly tall.

Seeing him standing on Ryan's doorstep was a punch to my gut. Jealousy rolled through me with the subtlety of a steam train. If I'd been a mood ring, I'd have been green with envy.

That could have been me.

I tore my gaze from the guy, calling myself ten types of stupid as I hit the accelerator.

Second chances only happen in fairy tales.

CHAPTER 3

Ryan

The call came through stupidly early.

"This is Ryan," I answered, scrubbing a hand over my face.

"It's Tristan. We got another arson attempt," the Sheriff sounded annoyed. "Can you take it?"

"Yep." I rolled out of bed and began searching for my pants. "Where'd they hit this time?"

"The old mill."

"Fuck." I paused in my dressing. "That's near the animal hospital."

"We already spoke to your brother. Apart from some nervous livestock and unsettled pets, there's no damage."

My eldest brother—and our father's only

biological kid—owned the town's Animal Hospital and Rescue Shelter. Hayden lived there with his wife, Kat—a photographer, and their three kids.

I made a mental note to flick him a text and drop by later to check-in.

"And the fire?" I asked, reaching for a heavy jacket.

"Nearly out. We'll be able to do assessments in the next few hours."

"Gotcha. I'm on my way."

"Thanks, Ryan. Keep me in the loop."

We hung up and I took a few minutes to dress before stumbling into the kitchen.

"Hey," Sam said, his voice rough. "You're up early."

"And you're up late," I said to my brother as I reached around him to snag the coffee pot. "The muse giving you a hard time?"

He nodded, cupping his mug of coffee. "This bridge won't quit. I can taste the melody but it just keeps dancing away when I try to get it down."

Sam—the youngest of my siblings but for our only sister, Janeane—breathed music. From the time he was young, he'd danced around the house singing into his hair brush and playing air guitar. Finally, Dad had given in and sent him off to music lessons expecting the fad to pass quickly.

Instead, Sam had surprised us all by becoming a musical prodigy, mastering eight instruments and crafting his own songs. Within a few years, he'd sold the songs to a bunch of musicians and joined a band. Now he spent part of the year in the Cove creating, and the rest of the time touring with his band.

Not bad for a twenty-three-year-old.

I finished filling my travel mug and turned off the machine. "I've got a job. You should get some rest before you pass out."

He lifted his hand and snapped out a teasing salute. "Aye, aye, Captain."

I rolled my eyes. "I'll catch you in a few hours."

He nodded, leaning his tall frame against the counter. "Be safe."

"Always."

The town was shrouded in mist as I rolled through the quiet streets, navigating my way out of the city centre and into the agricultural area that bordered the Cove.

I'd trained at university to become a structural engineer. My descent into investigations had come later after I'd volunteered as an emergency services officer. During a particularly bad storm season, I'd identified a few buildings that held a high degree of risk. The town's emergency services co-ordinator had recommended me to our police and fire services. The town had sponsored me to become certified as an investigator and now I was drawn on for any and all fire and storm issues.

I loved this job, I was good at it and it paid well. But the best part was that it allowed me to stay in the Cove close to my family and friends.

The sharp acrid tang of smoke wafted through the vents of my car, heralding the scene long before I arrived. Even this late in Autumn, the threat of fires remained alive. After a hot and humid summer, the land was ready for the rest that winter would bring—but we weren't quite beyond that threat just yet.

In the weak morning light, I could just make out the old mill structure—and the damage from the fire. A water-powered grist mill, the stone and wood structure had been closed up and roped off to the public decades ago when the original owners had sold the land. The current owners had left the structure to sit unused and unloved until the building had begun to crumble. It had become an attraction for local photographers, and a dangerous rite of passage for local teens.

Or it had been, I thought grimly as I observed the smouldering ruins.

I parked a little away from the two fire engines and just outside the barriers the local police had erected. I grabbed my camera, notepad, and pen from my bag.

Smoke hung heavy in the air, swirling through the mist like an unwelcome visitor. I paused a short way from the mill, snapping pictures. Through the crumbling brickwork, I could just make out the orange-red glow of dying embers.

"It's nearly out."

I turned to see Ren approaching. Tall and lean, the guy looked like he should be staring in movies rather than running the local fire department.

"Chief," I said with a nod, lowering my camera. "Any thoughts?"

Ren fell in beside me, crossing his arms over his chest. The wind teased his hair but he didn't seem to notice.

"Fire started on the north side of the building. Once it's out, we'll get you in to examine the structure."

I nodded, snapping another picture. "Deliberate?"

"Almost certainly. But we'll be able to confirm once we secure the scene."

"You mind if I walk the perimeter?" I asked, pulling my headlamp from my belt.

"Not at all. Just mind the bridge—damn thing looks like it's about to give way."

Help would no doubt arrive in the next few hours, but in the interim, I needed to secure the scene and ensure that any evidence was protected.

Switching on the headlamp, I pulled crime tape from my belt and began wrapping it around a tree. Pulling the tape with me, I slowly walked from one side of the structure to another, stopping here and there to secure the tape and capture pictures of anything that seemed out of the ordinary.

My job wasn't quite policing and it wasn't quite fire and rescue. It sat within an amorphous mixture of the two. My investigations required me to uncover how and why the fire or explosion occurred, whether a crime was involved, who might be liable, and how to prevent it from happening again. Because of my unique mix of skills, I'd become something of a national expert, travelling all over the country at the behest of insurance agencies and other regional fire departments to unpack crime scenes.

I brushed a stray ember from a tree, grinding it into the dirt with my boot.

I could have moved away years ago, but this was my home. It would always be my home because this is where I found my family and myself. It was where I felt safe, secure, loved.

It was where I belonged.

As dawn broke, the wind kicked up, bringing with it the cool bite of the coming season. Ash tumbled through the air peppering my clothes, skin, and hair with white and grey smudges.

I slowly made my way back to where the fire trucks were packing up.

"Ryan?"

My head snapped up, a shock of electric energy zinging from the top of my head to the tips of my toes.

"Trent?"

I didn't remember breaking a mirror, stepping under a ladder, tripping over a black cat, or putting my shoes on a table but it was quickly becoming obvious that my luck had changed—and not for the better.

For the second time in twenty-four hours, I stared at the man who had shattered my heart all those years ago.

"What are you—?" I trailed off, swallowing hard. Dressed in full gear, it was apparent he had joined our local brigade.

He glanced down at his attire—heavy boots, and turnout pants. His turnout coat with high-vis stripes had been left open providing me with tantalising glimpses of his regulation dark blue station shirt which clung to his muscular torso.

Must. Ignore. Temptation.

He took his helmet off, rubbing at a drop of sweat that decorated his forehead. He'd cut his hair since yesterday, the dark curls now tightly clipped.

"I transferred from Chars. Today's my first shift." Trent's lips quirked in a smirk fit to break the hearts of millions around the world. "Didn't expect to see this kind of action."

I fought for composure, desperately attempting to summon moisture into my dry mouth. For years I'd avoided all mention of him and now I couldn't seem to avoid him.

Story of my life.

He glanced at the camera and tape in my hands. "Are you a cop?"

I shook my head. "I'm a structural engineer but trained in investigations—including fire. The town doesn't have enough work or money to maintain specialised detectives or forensic experts, so they outsource to me when issues arise."

His eyebrow cocked. "Is there much of a demand for structural engineers in the Cove?"

I tried not to bristle at his question. "Enough to keep me fed."

I pointedly turned away from him, lifting my camera to snap another picture of the scene.

Did I need another picture?

No.

Did it prove to be a good distraction from Trent's hold over me?

Also no.

Why am I still attracted to him? The man broke my heart. There's nothing there. It's been nearly a decade, for goodness sake! There's no reason to still be this attracted to someone I barely know!

I glanced at Trent, unable to ignore the spike of lust warming my gut.

Maybe I just need a quick hook-up. I should call that guy I met in Haverston. Or reactivate a dating app or two.

I thought this knowing full well I wouldn't. I wasn't a hook-up kind of guy. I'd tried it once or twice but had quickly learned that I was a relationship person. I wanted deep connections and even deeper conversations. I wanted hand-holding and Sundays in bed.

I wanted someone to call mine. I wanted to belong.

I shook off my melancholy mood.

October always makes you morose.

October had been the month I'd finally been removed from my birth father's house. My birth father had been an addict and struggled with the addiction for most of his life. He'd been sober for five years now—his longest period to date. I didn't begrudge him his struggles. I'd made peace with him and myself years ago. And I couldn't complain about the incredible family I'd ended up with.

I'd bounced around the system for a few years before Will Dogg had become my foster father. He'd straightened me out, showering me with love, compassion, and support. The day my birth father had endorsed Will's adoption of me, had been one of the best I'd ever had.

But October always brought about the memories of being removed from my birth parent's home. Of the confusion and fear, the anger and uncertainty. No manner of therapy could dull that memory. You might process the emotion, but the memories would remain.

We stood in silence for a while, me snapping pictures I didn't need while he watched the smouldering scene, nursing a cup of steaming coffee.

His radio crackled and he reached up to murmur something into it.

"They're ready for you," he said, turning fully toward me. "But you might need a jacket... and a helmet." He placed a hand on the small of my back. "Come on. I'll get you sorted."

The heat of his hand burned through my

jacket to brand my skin. I slid away from his touch but followed him, avoiding lengths of flattened hoses and dirty equipment.

Trent pulled a helmet and spare jacket from one of the trucks, holding them out for me to take.

"Thanks," I muttered, begrudgingly, taking the jacket and trying to awkwardly shrug it on as I held my camera with one hand.

"Here." Trent stepped into my space, placing the helmet on my head with a wink.

I froze as he shifted, holding the jacket for me to step into. Our gazes met, and I saw something flash in his eyes—something warm and intimate and... yearning?

I dropped my head, pretending to fiddle with my camera.

"Thanks," I said gruffly. "We should get started."

We stopped by my car for a bag and then walked in silence down to the old mill, Trent allowing me to lead. Ignoring him became easier the closer we came to the scene, my mind ticking into work mode.

We stepped through the burnt shell of the mill and into the blackened interior. The fire had torn through the building, ravaging the old rotted beams and wood-panelled roof. A hole gapped large and ugly above us, smoke lazily swirling up toward the blue sky.

I began my examination, making notes on my pad as I toured the space. The beams that remained were corrupted, straining under the weight of what remained of the roof. The brick walls had overheated and showed evidence of cracks splitting across the ancient grout.

"We suspect the fire started over here," Trent said as I crouched beside the north wall.

I snapped some pictures of the burn pattern, frowning.

"No accelerant," Trent murmured. I glanced at him, raising an eyebrow.

"It's the burn pattern, right? Accelerant is normally narrow or even a U-shape if there's a puddle of gas or something. But this is wide."

I nodded. "If this is deliberate, they built it rather than doing a flash and run." I gestured at the char patterns streaking the wall. "If this was a hot, fast fire, I'd have expected to see lines with different burn rates. But what we have here is a slower burn."

I pulled a vapour detector from my bag and began to test the air, frowning when the detector came back with general readings.

"If there was an accelerant, the lab will need to detect it." I pulled a series of airtight containers from my bag, carefully labelling them before filling them with samples of ash, wood, and other debris from around the building.

"This is pretty fascinating," Trent said, watching me scoop small samples of ash from the different sides of the wall. "I haven't normally been involved in this aspect of an investigation."

"No?" I asked. "What did you do in Chars?"

"Mostly traffic accidents and medical emergencies. The structural fires we had were escalated up to the forensic investigators. But I guess a small town doesn't have the luxury."

I shook my head, carefully labelling the container in my hand. "It's a different pace here." I placed the final container in my bag and then glanced up at him. "You might find it boring."

His gaze met mine, unwavering. "You might be surprised."

A heartbeat passed, then another. Words unsaid swirled in the air like smoke, whispering across my skin and dancing across my lips.

I forced a chuckle, breaking our stare.

"I should get these to the lab."

"You need a hand?"

I shook my head, stubbornly determined to allow him no inch.

"Nah, I'm good."

I walked away from him, halting when he called my name.

"Ryan...."

I closed my eyes, savouring the sound of his voice.

"I'm back. For good."

I nodded once. "We'll see."

"Yeah," I heard him say as I walked away. "We will."

CHAPTER 4

Trent

I sat nursing a beer and a bad attitude at the town's local bar. Around me swirled people dressed in all manner of Halloween outfits, their costumes giving them license to be someone else—even if only for a few hours.

And I happened to be the schmuck sipping a beer and babysitting his sister and her housemate.

A woman sidled up to the table beside mine. From her sex kitten outfit and come-fuck-me-eyes, to the way her gaze kept sliding over my arms, she more than made her interest clear.

For a brief moment, I entertained the idea of

letting her talk me onto the dance floor and perhaps a little further, but quickly discarded the thought.

It had been a full week since I'd been back in town, and every second was pure, unadulterated hell.

Between living with my parents while I tried to source housing (something that wasn't easy in a small town), and my dick deciding the only person he'd wake up for was Ryan, I felt like I had regressed to my teenage years.

But worse than all that was Ryan. The one guy I want, the one guy my dick wanted, seemed to be doing everything within his power to avoid me.

"Tee!" Faye screamed in my ear, slamming into my side and jostling my beer.

Complete with pesky little sister.

I steadied her with one hand, frowning at her flushed face and overly-right eyes.

"Are you drunk?"

She made a dismissive wave. "Pshhh, no. At best I'm tipsy."

She swayed into me again, bumping her beaver-clad body into mine. Once upon a time, the only bar in town had been the Bronze Horseman. Now the owners had opened a swath of other venues, including this live music bar—and the whole month of October had Halloween Saturdays involving local and international acts, and costumes.

Ridiculous costumes.

"You're definitely drunk."

"Noooo," she protested, holding up one giant beaver foot. "It's these damned shoes. They're clumsy."

Heaving a silent sigh, I slid off my stool and helped her clamber onto it.

"Stay," I ordered sternly. "Let me find Hope and get some water into both of you. Then we're going home."

Faye's bottom lip slid out. "Booooooooo!"

I rolled my eyes, trying not to judge. "You can boo all you want, you're still going home."

"But the band—"

"Is wrapping up." I pointed at the stage where the lead singer was announcing their final song. "Hope, water, sleep."

She heaved a sigh. "If I must. Can we have ice cream on the way home?"

"Maybe."

She poked her tongue out at me. "Spoilsport. Hope's by the stage, if you're looking."

"Thanks. Be right back."

I made my way through the crowd, searching for my sister's best friend. For some reason, the housemates had decided to come as beavers. They'd giggled like a pair of toddlers in the back seat the entire way to the bar and had spent most of the night stumbling in their too-big beaver shoes.

I worked my way around the room, my mild annoyance turning to concern when I could locate Hope.

"Shit," I muttered as the band wrapped up their final song. "Where the hell is she?"

Making my way through the dancing throng of people, I began to search in earnest, my fear growing.

"Excuse me," I said, pushing between a banana and an apple. "Coming through," I said to an elf and Mrs Claus.

A hundred scenarios began to race through my head, each as horrible as the last.

Maybe she's in the toilet? Or perhaps she went outside for some fresh air. She could be at the bar or—

"Trent?"

I swung around, staring wide-eyed at Ryan. He was dressed as a Jedi, complete with a lightsaber and some weird alien pet attached to his shoulder.

How ironic that we should match.

"Hey." He reached out and placed a hand on my shoulder, his concerned gaze searching mine. "You okay?"

"Have you seen a beaver?"

He blinked slowly. "Um... is that a euphemism, a question about an animal, or a reference to a costume?"

"A costume."

"Not recently. I saw one by the stage a couple of minutes ago but—"

"Thanks." I spun away, intending to head back the way I'd come but his hand halted me.

"Wait. You seem stressed. Talk to me."

I hesitated, surprised by his question. My gaze dropped to where his hand rested on my arm.

I thought he hated me.

"My sister's roommate," I said. "She's missing. Faye's drunk so I can only assume she is as well and with all these people—"

"Say no more." Ryan straightened, raising on tip-toe to look out over the crowd. He raised a hand, gesturing at someone on the stage. The guy—the same one who'd been outside his house—saw him and waved back.

"Come on." Ryan grabbed my hand and pulled me along, tugging me up and onto the raised dais.

I tried not to relish the feel of his palm in mine.

"Sam, you remember Trent?" Ryan said, letting go of me as he introduced the good-looking guy.

And just like that, my pleasure evaporated.

A sucked in a breath, determined to force my way through the awkwardness of this interaction.

The guy wasn't living on pause while you gallivanted around the world.

I took Sam's outstretched hand and then froze. "Wait. As in Sam *Dogg*?"

Sam grinned, a slight flush touching his cheeks. "Yeah, I know. Puberty hit late."

My gaze raked over his body with new eyes. The last time I'd seen Sam he'd been short, skinny, and while his face had held the promise of good looks, puberty had yet to realise them.

That kid did not resemble the god before me.

I shook my head. "Faye used to be taller than you."

He rolled his eyes. "And didn't she used to hound me about it?"

"We're looking for a woman in a beaver outfit," Ryan said, his gaze running over the crowded bar. "And not the one currently chatting with the waitress over there."

My gaze snapped to where Faye and a waitress traded a laugh at my table.

"Oh, you mean Hope? She and Justice headed backstage. They're from the same small town." Sam shook his head. "Crazy coincidence, right? That's gotta be a punch line for a joke. Two Americans walk into a bar. One's a rock star, the other is dressed as a beaver."

Ryan ignored the tease. "You're telling me you let Justice Wild backstage with a woman?"

Sam cocked an eyebrow. "He's not a man-whore, Ry. Besides, she's dressed in the least sexy outfit I can imagine. How at risk do you think she's gonna be?"

"I intend to find out." Ryan headed for the backstage entrance. "Come on."

I trailed him, worried for Hope, guilty that I hadn't kept a better check on her, and strangely aroused by Ryan's heretofore unexpectedly bossy side.

We powered backstage, Ryan taking charge. We were quickly directed to a small room where most of the band and crew had assembled. They were swapping stories, sharing drinks, and there, in the middle of it all, sat a plump beaver in pigtails.

"Hope." I practically flopped with relief. "You're okay."

She tilted her head to the side, giving me a blank smile. "Of course I am. Why wouldn't I be?"

If she didn't realise then I wasn't about to inform her.

"Because you're drunk, honey." The lead

singer tugged gently on one of her pigtails. "Sounds like these nice guys are your ride home."

Her lower lip came out and I got a sense of déjà vu.

"But I want to—"

"Time to go," Justice ordered, not brooking any protests. He helped her scramble to her feet and pressed a small kiss to her forehead.

I had to look away when I saw the embarrassed flush creep up her neck.

Damn. The girl is crushing hard.

I glanced at Ryan.

I know the feeling.

"Off you go," Justice said, giving her a little shove in my direction. "We'll catch up another time."

Hope ducked her head and waddled out of the room, her beaver tail wobbling back and forth as we moved through the backstage area.

Ryan helped me collect a drunk Faye, scuttling her and Hope out to my car.

It took two of us to control my sister, who insisted on serenading half the town with her off-kilter singing.

"Thanks," I said shutting the door on her.

"I'd say any time, but my ears might not be able to take it," Ryan joked with a laugh.

He stood close enough that I could smell his

cologne and feel the heat of his body brushing my skin.

I lifted a hand to rub at the ache that bloomed in my chest.

"What?" he asked, his amusement fading as I stared at him.

"You've been avoiding me," the statement fell from my lips and landed between us

He pulled back. "I—you're—no, that's—"

"It's true. You're running all over the place trying to avoid me." I stepped closer to him, boxing him in against the car beside mine. "I want to know why."

His gaze widened, his face pale in the dim lights of the car park. "I... I'm not."

"No?" I reached up to cup his cheek, tired as fuck of the way he'd avoided me. "You sure? Cause I think," I stepped closer, forcing him to lean against the car behind him. "You're running scared."

His throat bopped as he swallowed. "You're mistaken."

"Really?" I leaned in, unable to silence the devil on my shoulder.

Just kiss him.

Faye broke the moment.

"Kiss or get in the car!" she yelled at me, hanging drunkenly from the car.

I sighed as Ryan slid out from beneath my arm, quickly high-tailing it across the car park.

"Coward," I yelled at his back.

"Coward?" He slid me a glance over his shoulder. "I don't go back for seconds. Ever."

And with that brutal but devastatingly effective return, he disappeared into the night.

"Damn," Faye drawled, half-slumped out of the car window. "That was harsh."

And with that, she leaned over and heaved the contents of her dinner onto the pavement.

I sighed wondering which mythical being I'd pissed off to deserve this level of karma.

CHAPTER 5

Ryan

My encounter with Trent played over and over in my mind until I became plagued by the idea that I was exactly what he had accused me of being—a coward.

It's not as if I hadn't wanted to kiss him. The spark, the attraction, the chemistry, the desire—it was all there.

But the need to protect my fragile heart outweighed the minor benefits a potential kiss might have offered me.

But damn. That kiss would be worth it.

I rolled over to punch my pillow once more.

I finally drifted into a restless sleep sometime in the early hours of the morning only to be woken what felt like five minutes later by the shrill tone of my cell.

Snatching it up, I squinted at the name on the screen and swore softly.

"Please don't tell me it's another one," I said, already swinging my feet over the side of my bed.

"I live to disappoint you," Ren replied sourly. "Whoever it is struck again. This time down at the old beach resort."

I closed my eyes, imagining the abandoned wooden structure being licked by flames.

"Well, at least we know their preferred target." I reached for my jeans. "Old abandoned buildings outside the main areas. Now we just need to figure out their motive."

"Teenage mischief?" Ren offered.

"No. If it was teens, they'd normally be building bigger fires. And we'd be likely to see fresh tagging so they can claim it."

"I have a favour to ask."

"Shoot," I said, cradling the cell between my shoulder and ear as I buckled my belt.

"As crap as these fires are, it's allowed Teddy and I to partition the city council to get more of our people trained in investigations. If you don't mind, I'll be assigning someone to tag along with you as you check out the fires from now on. I want them to see how you operate."

I frowned, reaching for one of my boots. "You planning on throwing me over?"

Ren chuckled. "Not quite. The town's growing. We're beginning to see increased incidents, and if we keep up with the pace we're running at, I expect we'll have more than enough work for you and at least a second investigator. You okay with helping train some others up?"

I considered his request. Another investigator would allow me to take on more of the insurance investigations—which frankly paid more than the town ever could.

"Sure," I said finally. "I'm sure I can teach one of your people how it's done."

"Great. Trent will meet you at the scene in an hour."

I blanched, coughing as the air caught unexpectedly in my throat.

"I'm sorry, did you say—"

"Shit."

I heard a siren wail in the background of Ren's call.

"Gotta go. Chat later," he hung up, leaving me to stare at my phone in shock.

Fuck.

Fuckity fuck fuck.

Fuckity mcfucking fuck fuckity fuck fuck.

I briefly contemplated messaging Ren to say I couldn't help, then tossed off that idea.

You are bigger than that.

Taking a deep breath, I finished lacing up my boots and grabbed my jacket.

The old beach resort had once been a thriving holiday destination for the nouveau riche of Astipia before it slowly became worn, dated and out of vogue. By the time the hippies had descended upon Lover's Lake and made their way down into Capricorn Cove proper, the resort had closed its doors, leaving behind all furnishings.

Teenagers had partied there for decades, drawn to the creepy time capsule. Featuring worn carpets, sand-infested curtains, and rich but decaying chandeliers, the old resort was the perfect place to make mischief.

And make-out.

I arrived at the resort and spotted Trent leaning against a parked truck. For a beat, I was transported back in time. A wave of bittersweet nostalgia washed over me.

Trent pressed me against a damp wall as candles and torches flickered down the hall. His lips had been warm and eager, his hands greedy as he slid one up my shirt and the other down my pants.

I shook off the memory, determined to ignore my racing heart as I approached him.

"Hey," he said, his voice gruff with sleep.

"Hey," I replied, trying to keep my tone casual.

We stood there in silence for a beat, seemingly unable to make conversation.

"Here." Trent reached behind him, pulling a coffee cup from a cardboard holder. "I got you some."

Inhaling the warm scent of cinnamon and nutmeg, I glanced at him over the rim of my cup. "You remembered?"

His gaze was warm. "Always."

I ducked my head and took a sip of the hot coffee. "Thanks. You didn't have to do that."

He shrugged as if remembering ten years later how I liked my drink wasn't a big deal.

Trent turned his attention to the smoking building. "They caught it early."

I hunched my shoulders, cupping my hands around the warm mug. The resort had been built to take advantage of the sweeping beaches and gorgeous views of the ocean. A gale had kicked up the night before, bringing with it rain and the chill of the coming winter season.

Leaves from ancient junipers that had been planted long ago swirled across the grass and sand lawns, tangling in overgrown hedges and wild tangles of naked branches.

The once white and blue buildings had faded to a muted grey, the paint flaking from worn wooden weatherboards, and rusted metal trims.

Trent and I fell into step beside each other, walking across the grounds in silent companionship.

He wore a lined black leather jacket, dark wash jeans, thick boots, and an expression that said he'd just rolled out of bed and would prefer to be back in it.

I hated that my gaze kept slipping toward him like a magnet being pulled toward a pole. I hated that I wanted to bring a smile to his face. I hated that I wanted to brush my thumb across his cheek and force him back to bed until those circles disappeared from under his eyes.

But mostly, I hated that I didn't hate him at all.

We made our way to the entrance of the grand hotel, ducking under the sagging roof and leaving footprints in the whisps of sand that had gathered on the old wood floors.

We stood blinking, our eyes adjusting to the dim interior light.

We made our way through the rickety building following the smell of salt, smoke, and burnt trash.

The hotel had been built around a central courtyard filled with a shrivelled garden, stinking pond, and cracked walkway.

"At least they did it outside this time," Trent muttered as we walked across the courtyard to where the remaining firefighters were standing.

Teresa "Teddy" Prince stood supervising a rookie as they sifted through the dying embers to ensure the blaze was completely extinguished. The dark-haired woman had quickly risen to the rank of Fire Chief, a position she shared with Ren.

She caught my eye, giving me a head lift.

"Ryan, Trent, good to see you." She gestured at the smouldering pile of melted trash and debris heaped in the centre of the courtyard. "You're welcome to sift through it, but I can already tell you it was an old bottle of turps that caused the damage."

Based on the way the half-melted bottle had stuck to the wall of the hotel, I had to agree.

"I'll give them credit," I said, dropping my bag to the ground and pulling my gloves free from my pocket. "Whoever it was doesn't look like they were intending to set the hotel on fire."

"Call came through about five this morning," Teddy said, beginning to gather some of their discarded equipment. "Panicked caller, pay phone, no name, young. Didn't stay on the line."

I frowned, crouching to begin laying out the

various items I'd need from my bag. "This doesn't look malicious."

"Mm. No sign of cars either. So, if it was kids, then it's someone local enough to be riding or walking home."

I felt Trent crouch beside me.

"What can I do?"

I forced myself to ignore the way his quiet question caused my heart to beat faster.

You have a job to do. Get to it.

"Start photographing the scene." I handed him my camera. "Take pictures of everything— wide shot, close up, all of it. You never know what might be of use."

He nodded, accepting the task without protest.

We worked quietly but efficiently, Trent shadowing me as I walked around the site, collecting samples and pointing out different patterns and areas to check. The others slowly left, leaving us alone to examine the scene.

"See this?" I asked, crouching beside a small bush. "What do you see?"

Trent frowned, examining the flattened grass and crushed leaves. "It looks like something rested here."

I nodded. "Based on the way the smaller grasses and plants are shaped, they only left a few hours ago."

"How can you tell?"

"Most will spring back when the sun rises." I gestured for him to take a picture, the scene taking shape in my mind. "I think I know what's going on."

"Mm?" Trent asked, snapping some shots.

"This isn't arson." I stood, grimly brushing dirt from my pants. "This is someone who needs help."

Trent raised his head, cocking an eyebrow. "How do you figure?"

"Abandoned buildings away from main areas. Fires on only the nights that have been cold. No accelerant or graffiti. No signs of vandalism or drinking or drugs."

I scrubbed a hand over my face. "I'm gonna go out on a limb and assume it's a kid."

My gut clenched as a myriad of memories assaulted me. Days spent searching for food, hiding from authorities, camping out on people's couches.

My heart ached for this kid, whoever they were.

"Why do you say that?" Trent asked, pulling me back.

I gestured at the small crushed space. "Adults would have the sense to stay inside. But a kid who might be scared of the dark?" I shook my head. "The hotel is a hundred percent guaranteed to scare the shit out of you—especially at Halloween."

Trent lowered the camera, his dark eyes catching mine. "Like that time we came here."

Memories swirled around us, filling the smoke-tinged air.

I forced a laugh, standing up. "Yeah. That was a long time ago."

Trent moved closer, his jaw tense, his eyes reflecting something deeper, darker, hungrier. I stood my ground, feeling like prey before a predator.

My belly dipped and for a minute I didn't know if I wanted to run, or grab him and never let go. I sucked in a breath, the acrid smoke seemly sweet compared to the memories of the things we'd left unsaid.

He broke the silence.

"I remember what you taste like," Trent's low rasp had a roughness to it that sent shivers down my spine. "I remember what you sound like as you come. How you used to grab onto the back of my neck as if you'd never let go."

I swallowed as desperate need simmered in my blood, an ache settling in my stomach.

Remember the hurt.

I broke our stare, glancing away. I swallowed against the desert that had settled in my throat.

"And I remember what it felt like when you broke up with me."

He blanched. "Excuse me? We *mutually* agreed to break up."

My head whipped back to stare at him. "What the fuck?"

He spread his arms out, glaring at me. "Are you really trying to lay all of that at my feet? You didn't even want to entertain the idea of leaving the Cove."

I blinked rapidly, my thoughts a jumble. "You never asked."

He reeled back as if I'd hit him. "Yeah, I did."

I shook my head vehemently. "No, you didn't. You told me you were going to Australia and that was it."

He stared at me, his eyes wide, his mouth moving up and down like a gasping fish.

"Ryan... what exactly do you think happened?"

The way he asked—with genuine interest and more than a touch of remorse— doused water on the flames of anger licking at my feet.

"You said you were going to accept the Australian scholarship and didn't think you'd return." I searched his face. "You then asked me what I was going to do. There was no asking,

Trent. No compromise. You had already made your decision."

He shook his head slowly. "Ryan... I wanted you to come with me."

"And I would have. But my family is here. Would I have travelled the world with you? Absolutely. But my heart is tied to the Cove." I shook my head and forced a smile. "But hey, this was all ten years ago. We've both moved on."

"I haven't."

CHAPTER 6

Trent

I didn't know why I'd said that. It made no sense. It's not as if I'd spend the last ten years of my life pining for Ryan. I'd had a life, relationships, experiences.

But a piece of you was missing.

I couldn't draw breath. The crushing weight of my mistake bore down on my chest.

He'd have come with me. If only I hadn't been so fucking stupid.

If, ifs were a wish, you'd still not own the world.

My mother's wise words settled my despair.

I couldn't change the past. But I had an opportunity to rewrite our future.

Ryan ran a hand through his hair over and

over causing the long strands to stick up in adorable tufts.

I curled my hand into a fist to keep from reaching for him.

"I...." he stopped, shaking his head. "I can't do this. Not here. Not now."

He bent to retrieve his things, fumbling with his tools as he tried to put them back in his bag.

With a heavy sigh, I dropped beside him, helping.

"I'm sorry," I said awkwardly, trying to soothe over the mess I'd made. "I didn't mean to start anything. You've got a life here. You've probably got a boyfriend or partner and I—"

"I don't," he interrupted. "Have someone, that is. I haven't in a long time."

Stunned by his admission, my mouth snapped shut. Ryan steadily avoided eye contact as we worked in silence clearing away his tools and samples and shutting down the scene.

I wanted to press him, but I let him have his space, somehow knowing that he needed the reprieve.

"Do you think they'll be back?" I asked as we loaded his truck with his equipment.

"Who?"

I nodded at the hotel. "The kid."

He paused, little frown lines marring his forehead.

"It's gonna be cold again tonight."

I scratched my chin. "Maybe we should leave them some food and a note?"

"Yeah. That could work."

I hesitated. "Perhaps a coat as well? Maybe a sleeping bag?"

He nodded. "Good idea. I'll pick up some things on the way to—"

"I'll help."

He froze, one foot in his car, the other on the rough gravel. "You don't have to."

My stubborn side came out. "I want to."

His gaze met mine, and I saw him searching my face for something. Whatever he was looking for, he must have found because he blew out a breath.

"Okay. I'll drop these off at the lab and meet you in town in an hour."

We separated and I couldn't help the little sizzle of anticipation that zipped down my spine.

A plan began to take shape.

Operation: Win back Ryan.

This wasn't about getting him to fall back in love with me—I was pretty sure that ship had well and truly set sail.

This was about rekindling our friendship. Did I want a romantic, passionate relationship with the man I was deeply attracted to?

Hell yes.

But that didn't mean I had a right to it.

And friendship with Ryan was a hundred percent better than what I currently had—which equated to crumbs from a table.

We met in town and began to wander Main Street, stopping in the camping store for a warm jacket, thick socks, and an insulated sleeping bag. At the grocery store, we each carried a basket as we toured the aisles, tossing in items like can openers, long-life milk, fresh fruit, and jars of peanut butter.

I held up a melon, testing its weight. "What do you think? If we added a small camp knife perhaps—"

Ryan's phone rang, interrupting me.

"No to the melon—they have no way to wrap the leftovers." He hit answer as I replaced the fruit in the display bin.

"James, hey." He turned slightly away from me, a small frown pinching his forehead. "Actually, I can't I'm—" Ryan sighed heavily. "Okay, okay. I'll drop some off in an hour. Fine, half an hour. Yeah, buddy, you do owe me."

He hit end, shaking his head as he slid his cell back into his pocket.

"Sorry, change of plans. I have to swing by James and Hazel's place and drop off some baby wipes and hydrolyte." He winced. "It seems that the kids are down with a little gastro."

"Damn. And with a new baby too."

"Yeah. Hazel's holed up in one of the bedrooms with the baby, while James looks after the other kids."

"How many kids do they have?"

"Four now. Genie is nearly four, the twins—Miles and Anthony—are two, and now little Liz."

I whistled. "That's a lot of kids in a short period."

"I know." Ryan led the way to the baby aisle. "But they do a great job. James is an incredible dad, and Hazel is the kind of mum everyone should grow up with. Despite having more money than a small country, they're pragmatic about their parenting."

I watched him search through the aisle for the elusive wipes. "They're part of the reason the Cove started expanding, right? Something to do with a battery?"

Ryan nodded. "Ash designed a fully eco-friendly battery. It kick-started their company and now they're in renewables, saving the planet one genius invention at a time."

"That's pretty cool." I found the hydrolyte and tossed a few packets into my basket. "But you didn't go into the business?"

He shook his head. "They offered to find me a position but it wasn't a good fit. I prefer what I do. It gives me purpose and for other things."

"Other things?" I asked, trailing him up to the checkout.

"Mm. Surfing, photography. That kind of stuff."

I groaned. "You still surf?"

He chuckled. "Of course. I take it you still have zero balance on water?"

It sucked to admit it since we'd grown up next to the coast, but I was a terrible surfer. The water hated me, the board regularly knocked me out, and let's not get into the number of times I'd ended up half-drowned or nibbled on by a shark.

"The less said about my surfing fails, the better."

We paid for the supplies and then walked out to the car park, falling into an easy silence.

"Ah shit," I groaned, dropping the bags next to my truck. "I thought it'd felt off on the drive back to town."

My front left tyre had deflated and a quick feel of both sides found the culprit, a pesky screw.

I glanced at my watch, silently cursing.

"Tyre shop will be closed," Ryan confirmed,

placing his bags beside mine. "But if you have a spare, we can swap it out."

"I don't. The damn thing didn't come with one and my order isn't due until next week."

He winced in sympathy. "Ouch."

We both remained crouched by the tyre, an awkward tension descending.

"If you don't mind a few detours, I could drive you home," Ryan finally offered.

I hesitated, unsure of how genuine his offer was. "I wouldn't want to put you out."

"Tee, I'm trying to do something nice here. Take the damn offer."

Surprised and delighted by his unexpected use of my nickname, I accepted his offer.

Piling our shopping into his car, we chatted amicably as he drove through the streets towards Millionaire Row.

"Hazel prefers their house by the lake, but they like to stay closer to town for the weeks when James has to work in the office." He shot me a grin. "Or when they've just had a baby and need some extra hands."

The houses around us were towering mansions hidden behind ornate fences and even more ornate gardens.

Once upon a time, the land around Capricorn Cove had been filled with fishermen and their families. While there had been those who had vacationed in the area, most of the rich hadn't bothered to put down roots.

But as the cities that flanked either side of the Cove had slowly grown, those looking for weekend escapes had discovered our quaint town, buying up prime (and cheap) real estate and building odes to their wealth.

"I'm surprised James decided to settle in this part of the Cove," I said, frowning as we glided further along.

"Unfortunately, he and Ash are now at the stage of wealth where they need protection. Bodyguards, electric gates. Someone tried to snatch Genie from daycare last year. Hazel about lost her mind, and James purchased this house the next day."

"That's horrible."

He sighed. "That's life as a billionaire. My brothers are brilliant, and they're changing the world for the better. But with that comes re-sponsibilities that attract people who want to use them for their own advantage." He shook his head. "I worry, especially about the kids."

He hit the indicator and turned into a drive-way. "But despite the downsides, you can buy places like this."

The gates swung open at the press of a code and we drove down a long, winding driveway toward a lovely older home. Built in the Hampton's style, the house featured multiple decks, lots of windows, and beautiful crisp paint.

We parked at the end of the drive and I noted that while the land around us was large, the house itself was modest.

I mentioned that to Ryan as we walked to the door and he laughed.

"Looks can be deceiving. They have eight bedrooms and three bathrooms—but with four kids and a plethora of family who love to stay here, they need all the room they can get."

The door flew open before Ryan could twist the knob. James Dogg bounced one child on his left hip while another clung to his back, their small arms around his neck as they wailed loudly. A third child clung to his right leg, big tears falling down their tiny face.

I stepped back as a wave of smell assaulted my nostrils.

"Shi—I mean," Ryan coughed. "Shoot. You stink."

"Both twins need changing. Genie just vomited all over her bed, and I'm pretty sure the baby peed on me before I put her down to sleep."

Ryan handed me the bag he'd been carrying and held his arms out to take a toddler.

"Come on, let's get you all cleaned up."

A liquid heat unlike any I'd experienced slid

through my veins as I watched Ryan tease, prod, and poke the family into a better mood.

The children were all sent for a bath while James and I stripped beds and put on loads of washing. Ryan handed out ice blocks and checked temperatures, made up songs, and soothed hurt feelings.

He was magnificent, and I'd let him slip away.

What the hell had I been thinking?

CHAPTER 7

Ryan

"Anthony is bad," Miles told me, his little face flushed.

"Is he?" I asked, tucking my nephew into his bed. "Why's that?"

"He hit me."

I frowned. "In play or was he angry?"

Miles rubbed a fist against his eye—a sure sign he was exhausted. "Angry."

"I don't know."

"Did he apologise?" I asked, running a hand over his soft hair.

"Yes."

"Did you forgive him?"

He shook his head.

"Why not?"

"Cause he hurt me."

I smiled. "Sometimes people hurt each other when they're upset. Did he sound sincere when he apologised?"

He nodded.

"Then maybe you should forgive him."

"Is that what you do?"

I opened my mouth, then snapped it shut.

If I was honest with Miles and myself, no. I hadn't forgiven Trent. He'd long ago apologised for hurting me, but I'd frozen him out.

I still was.

Damn.

"Not all the time," I answered honestly. "But I try. Think you can do the same?"

"What if he hits me again?"

I ruffled his hair. "Sometimes you have to take a chance that it'll all work out."

Miles sighed heavily. "O-tay, Uncle Ry."

I kissed his forehead. "Try and get some sleep, champ. You'll feel better tomorrow."

I finished tucking Miles into his bed, then peeked in on my other wards. All the children were finally asleep, everything was clean and somewhat tidy, and James and Hazel appeared to be napping.

All was right in my world—except for the mind-blowing realisation that perhaps life was as simple as forgiving Trent.

I leaned my head against the hall wall, searching my feelings.

The top was—and probably would always be—overt attraction. But if I truly searched my heart, I didn't hate him. Hell, I wasn't even disappointed by him. We'd been kids. Mistakes happen, people get hurt, and people grow and move on.

Carrying a grudge for the past ten years hadn't served anyone.

"Shit," I muttered, chuckling to myself. "I guess I'm growing up."

I wandered back out to the kitchen and stopped as a kaleidoscope of butterflies took flight in my stomach.

Trent stood at the stove, his shirt off (Anthony had vomited over him), wearing an apron and stirring something that smelled suspiciously like Bolognese.

Hello, God? It's me, Ryan. I know you don't grant wishes but....

He turned back to the counter, catching sight of me. His hair was still damp from his rushed shower, and a small drop of water sat at his temple.

I found myself fighting the urge to lick it away.

"Hey," he said softly, scooping up some fresh herbs. "Are they down?"

I nodded, mentally rolling my tongue back into my head. "For now."

He tossed the herbs into the pot and gave it a little stir before turning the heat down.

"You didn't have to stay," I said, sliding onto one of the bar stools.

He lifted one powerful shoulder in a half-shrug, the muscles across his back rippling deliciously. "It goes against the oath to abandon someone in need."

I chuckled, reaching for a bottle of wine. "You want some?"

He eyed the label. "Go on then. Only a half glass, though. We still have to drive."

I poured one for each of us and set them on the counter, watching him take a slow sip.

Sometimes you have to take a chance that it will all work out.

My words to Miles circled my head, and I recognised that I had two options. I could continue to keep Trent at a distance or take a chance that maybe this lingering attraction could be the start of something new. Something different. Something better.

Maybe it would all work out this time.

I cleared my throat. "We should start again."

Trent raised an eyebrow over his glass.

"We're not who we were. And...." I forced

the words out. "I'd like to get to know who you are now."

He crossed his arms over his chest and leaned back against the counter, a small smile playing at the corner of his lips. "Oh really?"

I shot him a look. "Don't play coy, Tee."

He chuckled, dropping his hands and coming around the counter to take the seat beside mine. He slid a hand onto my knee, resting it there.

"I'd like that. A lot."

His gaze dropped to my lips. "And as much as I want to restart a relationship with you, I'm happy with where we're at. I just want you back in my life—however I can get you."

Take a chance.

I leaned in. "And if I want more?"

His eyes widened. "More as in...?"

Taking a chance, I wrapped a hand around the back of his neck and pulled him gently toward me. "As in this."

My lips brushed over his in a teasing caress.

I'd meant to keep it light. Soft. Teasing.

I'd meant to be making a point about... something?

What was my point?

I couldn't remember but it certainly wasn't pulling away only to have Tee fist my shirt and haul me in for a deeper, longer, hotter kiss.

Trent, it seemed, liked to be in charge.

And that was my last thought that went beyond, 'Oh, yes' and 'Please, more'.

He slid from his seat to wedge himself between my legs, changing the angle of our kiss.

His mouth tugged at mine, his teeth grazing my lower lip. A moan rumbled in my throat, desperate and rough.

So much for taking things slow.

He tasted of wine and decadence. My hands drifted down, slipping beneath the soft fabric of the apron to run over the solid steel of his chest.

Desire flared in my belly, my cock straining against the zipper of my jeans.

I needed more.

My lips slid from his to pepper kisses down his cheek, across his neck, and down to his collarbone. My teeth grazed his shoulder as he pushed me closer, seeming to need the same pleasure-pain I burned to deliver.

"Yessssss," Tee hissed as I sank my teeth into his skin. "Harder."

Sucking and biting, I marked him, branding my need into his tender flesh.

And he returned the favour, tugging at my hair and scoring nails down my back.

I pulled away only to return to his mouth, meeting him in a hungry, desperate kiss.

Our tongues tangled, dancing and stroking

as he tasted me and I tasted him, building the desire between us.

There was an art to our seduction that hadn't been there before. An edge that came with confidence, experience, and the understanding that life had sought to reunite us.

I shoved the apron up to his waist, my hands fumbling with his belt.

To what end, I'd never know for a cough interrupted our frantic make-out session.

We pulled back, both of us twisting to see James standing in the doorway, his head tilted back as he stared at the ceiling, a slight flush on his cheeks.

"Sorry," he said, sounding amused rather than apologetic. "But I thought you may want this."

He held up Trent's cleaned shirt, having run it through the washer and dryer.

Reluctantly, I let Tee go, allowing the apron to fall and cover his abs.

I never thought I was an abs man.

He awkwardly walked across the room to accept his shirt from James, both of them avoiding eye contact.

James cleared his throat. "Thanks for sticking around. I know you guys had other things to do tonight."

"Speaking of." I slid from my seat and

pulled down my coat, attempting to hide my erection. "We should get going."

Tee removed the apron and tossed it on the counter before tugging on his shirt. My belly did a little flip-flop watching him.

"Let the sauce simmer for another ten minutes, then you can let it cool and freeze it," he told James.

"Appreciate it." He slapped a hand on Trent's shoulder. "Seriously."

By unspoken agreement, we made only small talk as we drove to the hotel and dropped off our package for whoever was living there.

"Where to?" I asked, idling the car when we were done.

"Um, my parents."

I raised an eyebrow, a smile playing at the corners of my lips. "I'm sorry?"

Trent sent me a scathing look. "Don't make fun. It's only temporary."

I chuckled, putting the car into drive. "Mmhmm."

"I mean it. Besides, they could use the help." He shook his head.

I sobered. "Is that why you came back?"

"Partly." He heaved a heavy sigh. "They're getting older and the house is starting to get a bit much for them. Asking Faye to shoulder that burden by herself would be selfish." He trailed off, staring down at his hands in the dark.

"You don't have to tell me," I said softly. "It's okay."

"No, I want to." He twisted in his seat to face me more fully. "I left because I felt like staying would be a prison. I didn't feel free to be who and what I am. But leaving didn't bring me peace. I searched the world, trying to find my space in it." He huffed out a bitter chuckle. "Turns out I could have used a few months of therapy to tell me what ten years of searching failed to show."

I hit the indicator, turning down Main Street. "And that is?"

He gestured at the buildings we were driving past. "That this was never the problem." He placed a hand on his chest. "I was."

I frowned. "In what way?"

"I had never reconciled who I was and what I wanted."

"And you have now?"

He nodded. "Yeah."

"I'm glad." I pulled into his parent's driveway. "The worst thing in life is failing to know and be true to yourself."

I parked the car. "So you're back for a time or...?"

He shook his head. "I'm back for good." He nodded at his parent's house. "I no longer see this as a prison. It's a home. A resting place. I can still have the adventures, but having the familiar to come home feels good."

I tried to reconcile what I knew of past Trent with the man beside me. As a teenager, he'd had itchy feet, keen to escape the doldrums of our small town. But the man beside me had undergone a fundamental shift.

"Your therapist must have been excellent."

"She is," he chuckled. "She reminded me that unless I'm comfortable with my own identity, I'll never be comfortable in this world. And just like that, everything clicked."

I placed a hand on his knee. "I'm sorry you didn't feel like you could be your true self."

"Thank you." He slid a thumb across the back of my hand. "And I'm sorry if I ever made you doubt your value."

"Thank you," I said through a lump in my throat.

We sat quietly for a moment, the shadows of the night gently swaying over the darkened interior of the car.

"You want to come in?" he asked, his voice husky.

"Though the front door or your window?" I asked with a laugh.

His lips quirked. "Think you could still climb up the gutter?"

I glanced over at his house, measuring the distance from the ground floor to his second-floor bedroom.

"Not a chance," I said cheerfully. "But in answer to your question." I withdrew my hand from his reluctantly. "No. I need to get back and write up my report while it's still fresh."

He nodded, his face falling.

"But," I said, taking a chance. "We could do dinner tomorrow night."

His lips spread into a slow, sexy grin. "We could do that."

"Dancing?" I asked, knowing how much I wanted to press my body against his.

"Are you looking for an excuse to touch me, Mister Dogg?"

I leaned across the console. "And if I am?"

He moved in until our foreheads brushed. "Then I might let you."

His lips were warm and gentle. This wasn't a passionate explosion but a slow, lingering promise of what was to come.

"Good night, Ryan."

He exited the car and I waited, watching until he disappeared inside.

Blowing out a long breath, I shook my head.

"That man is dangerous."

Smiling with delight, I couldn't stop the shimmer of anticipation. And, honestly, I didn't even want to try.

CHAPTER 8

Trent

I captured Ryan's hips in my hand, pulling him into me with a sharp tug. He didn't complain as the band kicked up the rhythm, belting out a bone-pounding chorus.

I'd spent the day at the station where our only call out had been for Mrs. Anderson's dog, which had gotten its head stuck in a length of pipe. Stephen, the goodest of good boys, had been successfully released and was now recovering from his ordeal by snacking on treats and receiving pats from his grateful owner.

Clocking off had given me just enough time to race home, get clean, drop off my parent's car (mine was still in the shop waiting on the new tyre) and experience an overwhelming amount of anxiety related to tonight.

The anxiety had all been for naught. Ryan and I fell into an easy back-and-forth, sharing life stories, and laughing about old memories. Ten years had granted us both enough experiences to keep the dinner entertaining.

One course had turned into two then three. The band had started up, and before I knew it, we were dancing, our arms wrapped around each other, our heads pressed close together.

My hands slid over him, his lips grazing my cheek as we moved in time to the music. Our hips pressed before sliding away, our arms holding on for a beat too long, our legs tangling a time too many.

Ryan had exquisite control of his body. He moved fluidly, his limbs a graceful extension of the music. Our gazes met, holding.

I wanted him. And I had a feeling he wanted me, too.

The song ended and I pulled Ryan close, nipping my teeth into his earlobe.

"Let's get out of here," I murmured into the shell of his ear. "I need to taste you."

He caught my hand, leading me through the crowd and outside to his car at the far end of the dark lot. He pressed me against his truck, my back hitting the metal with a dull thud. I ignored it, caught between pleasure and pain as he feasted on my mouth. Our hands were entities unto themselves, slipping under clothing to run up each other's torso, fisting hair or playing frantically at the other's belt.

Ry—it appeared—had planned this. He'd parked next to the high wooden fence that circled the lot, picking a shadowed space far away from curious eyes.

"Need to—"

Ry's groan matched my own as he slipped his hand into my pants, wrapping his fist around my cock.

"Ry, wait. Ryan, we can't—" I jerked my hip forward, my head tilting back as he took control.

Dropping to his knees, he tugged my pants down until his hot mouth could encircle my straining dick.

"Fuck!

The man knew how to pleasure me, working my cock deep into his throat and then pulling back to tease the crown. One of his hands fisted my length while the other massaged my balls.

Ryan ignored my half-hearted protests—his confidence was a goddamned turn-on.

"Fuck, baby," I groaned, my hips thrusting

me deeper into his mouth. "Fuck that feels good. Keep going."

He ignored my direction and slowed down, pulling back to lick slow, wet circles around my head and down my length.

"Tee?"

"Yes?" I panted, seconds away from holding him still while I fucked his mouth raw.

"Shut the fuck up." He looked up at me, his eyes glinting dangerously in the moonlight. "This time, I'm in control."

I nearly came.

I've died and gone to Stern Brunch Daddy heaven.

This was a side of Ryan I'd never had a chance to experience. Our adolescent couplings had been passionate but filled with naivety. We hardly knew more than how to get each other off. The majority of my time with him had been stolen afternoons in the hour between school letting out and my parents returning home from work.

We'd been panicked and horny, frustrated and frantic. Insatiable in our urge and need.

The creature kneeling at my feet had no such issue.

He was made of steel and experience, willpower and control—the combination was intoxicating.

"If you insist." My fingers loosened on his hair, and I forced myself to relax as he leaned forward, running his tongue over my length in a torturously slow lick.

He murmured praise as he worshipped my dick, the heat of his mouth and hands a painful contrast to the cool night air.

"Fuck, I'm close," I admitted, fighting to hold out against his erotic onslaught.

Ryan growled around my dick, his finger dipping to find my taint.

With a yell, the first hot spurt of my cum splashed across his tongue. I moved to pull back but his hands held me to him, his mouth hot and tight around me as he rode out my orgasm.

I slumped back against the car, grateful when he surged to his feet to gather me in a warm embrace. Tiny kisses peppered my neck and cheeks as he gently restored my clothing.

"What about you?" I asked, surprised to hear a slight slurring of my words.

Sex drunk. I'm sex drunk.

"Later," Ryan promised, reaching around me to open the car door.

"Later?" I asked hopefully, allowing him to pour me into the passenger seat.

He pulled on my seat belt, clicking it in place as if I were a toddler. Taking advantage of his position, he turned his head, capturing my lips in a long, languid kiss.

"Mm," he hummed, pulling back slowly. "Let me get you home."

With a sigh, I closed my eyes, sinking into his car seat.

"Damn," I muttered, crossing my arms over my chest. "I wasn't ready for tonight to end."

It wasn't until we pulled into his driveway that I realised he wasn't either.

Home –it seemed—meant his place.

He turned off the car, the silence filling the interior.

After a beat, Ryan cleared his throat. "Sorry, I shouldn't have assumed you'd want to—"

I burst into motion, leaning across the console to silence his mouth with a punishing kiss.

CHAPTER 9

Ryan

Trent tasted of wine and chocolate, of sweat and heat, of desire and madness.

For this was madness, this need that he evoked within me. It sizzled through my veins, heating my skin and setting my world a flame.

My porch light switched on and Trent and I sprang away from each other.

"Yo," Sam called, raising a hand in hello as he carried his guitar out to his car. "I'm off to record some tunes with Justice." He tapped a knuckle against my driver's window as he passed. "Hi, Trent. Have a fun evening, you two."

Blushing, I unclipped my seat belt, avoiding Trent's amused gaze.

"This feels like high school all over again," he said as Sam pulled away.

I sighed. "Did he ruin the mood?"

Trent's lips quirked in a half-smile. "The opposite, actually. With the house empty...." He trailed off, and I finally met his gaze, registering the overt heat shimmering in his eyes.

"Inside?" I asked, my voice low and deep.

"Absolutely."

In silent agreement, we exited the car, walking close but not touching. It was as if we both knew that one graze would ignite the painful tension simmering between us.

I pushed open my front door, holding it aside for Trent. He stepped through, the dim light of the hall barely penetrating the darkness of the room.

I'd purchased the small bungalow a few years prior. It wasn't anything special—just a three-bedroom, one-bath build with a large yard and small living space. In winter, the interior was slightly too cold, and in summer, it ran slightly too hot. The paint was worn, and the floorboards were scuffed. The bathroom had lime-green tiles with mermaids, and the kitchen had once been a bright yellow that had faded to an unappealing creamy tangerine.

It needed work, repairs, insulation—but it was home.

My home.

My inner child rejoiced in the stability and security it represented every time I walked through the front door. Growing up in transient housing where each day could have been the start of another move, I relished the opportunity to own something permanent. Something that was holistically and totally mine.

"This house suits you," Trent said, running a hand along a low wooden bookshelf.

My lips quirked. "Are you saying I'm also a fixer-upper?"

His gaze met mine and my amusement faded.

"You're not a fixer-upper. You're perfect just as you are."

A lump formed in my throat.

"And this?" He waved a hand around to encompass the space. "This is a house that has roots. It's settled. This neighbourhood is the kind of place where you come when you want to create a family, be part of the community, grow old."

He knocked a knuckle against the wall. "Sure, she needs a little TLC. But I can see why you bought her."

"And that is?" I asked, my voice strangely hoarse.

He smiled. "You want the continuity she represents."

I opened my mouth but found myself unable to deny his statement.

He stepped into my space, crowding me back against the door. "I like this house for you."

But would you like it for you?

I wanted to ask the question burning on the tip of my tongue. I wanted to know if this was the kind of place he could see himself settling into, building out, renovating, and living in.

If he could see himself doing all of that with me.

He cupped my cheek, his gaze warm. "I know what you're asking Ryan—I can see it in your eyes. And the answer is—yes. I spent ten years wandering the world, trying to find my place in it. And this whole time, it turns out, it was right where I started." He kissed my cheek. "My place is beside you."

I gripped his hips, holding him away from me. "Don't lie to me, Trent. I'm a big boy, I can take it. If this is just a fling, you can—"

He interrupted me with a soul-stealing kiss. His lips were hot and demanding, his hands fierce as he hauled me against him.

"This. Is. No. Lie," he grunted between hungry kisses. "Bedroom. Now."

We stumbled our way through the house, crashing into walls, doors and furniture, tipping over picture frames and knocking potted plants.

We didn't stop as this grasping, gasping, shivery need drove us.

He slid his tongue into my mouth and I couldn't stop my bone-deep groan. Moving him down my hall, I shoved him into my bedroom then pinned him against my wall, rocking my hips into his.

His erection pressed against my leg as I ground against him. Our kiss is deep, hungry, desperate.

I'm dying.

I want Trent more than I've ever wanted anyone or anything in my life. I'm aching with need. Throbbing with desire.

He let out a moan, rocking harder into me.

"Fuck," I barked, pulling away a fraction.

His eyes blinked open, searching my gaze as his tongue playfully licked my lips. "You better not be stopping."

I choked out a spluttered exclamation. "Fuck no."

"Good."

His hand slid across my chest to wrap around my neck. "Take my pants off."

I fumbled at his belt, eager to taste him once more.

This time, our roles are reversed. He's in control, directing my movements while I'm a fumbling mess.

"Now you." He whipped off his shirt and discarded it lazily, watching as I did the same—with a distinct lack of finesse.

We stumbled backward and tumbled onto the bed, rolling until we were side by side, legs entangled, and chests pressed together.

Trent was heat and strength, silky skin over steel abs. We ground together in hungry, filthy movements until I couldn't bear it anymore. I spat in my palm, then slipped a hand between us to grip our cocks.

"Fuck," he gasped as I stroked down my shaft and up his.

Our gazes locked as I fisted us.

"You're so goddamned hot," he growled, one hand gripping my hip, the other wrapped around the nape of my neck.

I squeezed his cock a little harder. "You're not bad yourself."

Trent wiggled. "My turn."

Letting go of me, he shuffled down the bed, kissing his way down my body until I burned with tight need.

My cock pulsed as his hot breath danced

across my overly sensitised skin, sending shimmers of pleasure up my shaft. My balls drew tight as he gently pushed me over until I lay on my back.

"Let me play."

Unable to refuse his whispered request, I rested one hand on his shoulder, the other fisting my bedsheets.

Don't come. Don't come. Don't come.

If this was going to be my one chance, I needed to make this last.

I knew what Trent had said about staying in the Cove, but there was still a part of me that doubted his words. When he'd left, he'd fractured off a piece of my trust.

That didn't mean I wasn't willing to take a chance. It just meant I was prepared to hold a little hope back.

I didn't know if this made me an optimist, pessimist, realist, or some other 'ist', but I was pretty sure Trent wrapping his mouth around my cock had made me the luckiest at that moment.

His hot mouth worked my cock, slowly taking me deeper and deeper. One of his hands gripped the base of my shaft, holding me steady while the other toyed with my balls, driving me wild.

I was hot, shivering, and aching with need.

Don't come, don't come, don't come.

He growl, forcing me further down his throat, his gaze locked with mine as he sucked me hard.

"Fuck, I'm gonna—"

Rather than pull away, Trent doubled down, working me harder, faster, wetter.

I arched my hips, fisting his hair. "Fuck, baby. That's it. Harder, Trent. Yeah, like that. Fuck. Fuck, I'm gonna—"

I came, and he swallowed my cum greedily, licking and sucking until I was completely spent.

I collapsed back on the bed, blinking up at the dark ceiling as I wondered if I'd died and gone to orgasm heaven.

"Shit," Trent said, rolling over and jacking his dick roughly. "That was hot as fuck."

I blinked, pulling myself together.

"You want me to—" my question was cut off as he came over his stomach with a long, low groan. "Help," I said with a chuckle. "I guess you didn't need me after all."

He slumped against me, his lips finding my shoulder. "I would have said yes but I was too close to wait. Besides, you've already gotten me off once tonight."

I bit my tongue as I contemplated how he'd

feel about an offer for another round or five hundred.

We lay beside each other for a moment, staring into each other's eyes as we caught our breath.

This felt familiar and different, the same and yet not. There was comfort here, but also so much about him that had changed that everything felt new and exciting.

Maybe he'll stay this time. Maybe he'll—

"I better clean up. Where's your bathroom?"

I pointed at the ensuite door. He left to clean up, while I rolled onto my back and slung an arm over my eyes, silently berating myself for my thoughts.

Jesus, Ry. You've blown each other once and you're already thinking about picking out rings and paint colours? Slow the fuck down, dude.

Trent returned a few minutes later carrying a pack of condoms, lube, and a towel.

I cocked an eyebrow. "I thought you were cleaning up."

"I was." He tossed the items onto my bedside table. "But then I found your stash and decided it might be worth hauling it in here."

That tiny part of me I'd been withholding, shook a little as I tried—and failed—to suppress my smile. "Who said you're staying tonight?"

He fell onto the bed, wrapping his arms around me and nuzzling into my chest. "Oh, I'm staying."

I slipped a hand under his chin to tilt his head back, meeting his gaze. "What if I said no?"

His eyes flashed with heat at my teasing tone. "I guess I'd have to try and convince you otherwise."

My cock—idiot that it was—began to pay attention.

"Well then," I said, rolling us over until he was pinned under me. "Convince me."

With a filthy curse, he got to work.

CHAPTER 10

Ryan

I waited at the bar, fiddling with the fake glasses I wore on my nose.

Around me swirled a couple dressed as the leads from *Rocky Horror Picture Show*, a llama, a chef, and a woman whose costume was so obscure I couldn't understand it.

"She's embodying 'Solar Eclipse of the Heart'," Trent said, his lips brushing the shell of my ear.

I grinned, leaning back against him. "How do you figure?"

He slid a drink into my hand and wrapped his arm around me. "The heart painted like the sun with the moon half covering it."

"Ah, that makes more sense."

He kissed my neck. "What did you think it meant?"

"Something to do with a full moon. Like fated mates or something."

He chuckled, his warm breath teasing my sensitive skin. "Do you believe in fated mates?"

I chewed over his question, buying myself time by taking a sip of my drink.

"Not in the way you might think."

He pulled back a little and turned around so we were face to face.

"Go on," he prompted, leaning against the bar.

"I believe in soul mates as someone who makes up the other half of you. But I don't believe they have to be romantic. They *can* be a lover, but they might be a sister, a friend, or even a pet. A fated mate, meanwhile, isn't something I believe in. I think someone becomes your fated mate because you grow together. You start as two separate beings and slowly, intrinsically, become so intertwined that you cannot separate one from the other. It isn't fate—which implies a lack of choice and growth—it is you deciding to grow together. It's you and your partner choosing each other again and again until the choice becomes so ingrained, so automatic, that there is no choice. There's only you and them together."

I huffed out a laugh, shaking my head. "Too deep, right?"

"No," Trent said, wrapping his hand around the back of my neck and pulling me to him. "It's beautiful."

He kissed me softly, lingering for a beat too long in such a crowded place. Around us, people called out orders, chatted loudly, or swayed in time to the music. This moment shouldn't have been romantic. It shouldn't have been intimate. But we were caught in our own little bubble, as if a forcefield had wrapped around us, cocooning us from the chaotic cheerfulness of the bar.

I rested my drink on the wooden countertop and wrapped my arms around his middle, sliding my hands into the pockets of his tracksuit pants.

We'd dressed as our first crushes—I'd come as Clark Kent, while Trent had surprised me by dressing as Zac Efron's character from High School musical. I had no idea where he'd found the Wildcats outfit but I couldn't deny he looked great dressed as a jock.

The grey sweats also didn't hurt.

"How firm are you about staying for the band?" he asked, pressing his groin into mine.

"I promised Sam...." I said, tilting my head

back as his teeth grazed my collarbone. "Maybe we could skip out after the first set."

Trent growled.

"Or... earlier?"

"Better." With a heavy sigh, he let me go. "Don't look at me until you're ready to go, or I'll haul you over my shoulder."

I chuckled. "As if you could—"

"Don't tempt me."

I eyed him, mentally calculating his strength.

"Ryan." He gave me a stern look.

Poking my tongue out, I spun back around, rocking back into him as Sam and his band walked onto the stage.

The Wild Ones were slowly carving out a name for themselves in the business. They'd opened for Wolf Rodriguez last year and re-leased a successful single last month. I didn't doubt that my brother and his friends would be selling out stadiums in the future—if they could keep the band together.

They kicked off their first set, thumping out an epic rock-pop number before flowing into another, then another.

Within minutes, Tee and I were dancing, our hips pressed together, our hands clinging as we fell in with the crowd.

A feeling I'd not experienced for several

years slowly stole over me, seeping out from my marrow and into my bloodstream until every inch of my was coated in its golden glow.

Joy.

The pure joy that only love brought.

In the space between two beats, my heart toppled, the remains of the walls I'd erected crumbling to dust.

There was no escaping us.

And I didn't want to. I wanted to do exactly as I'd described—grow together into some new and unique being. I wanted to be so intertwined that there was only us.

I caught his hand and led him from the dance floor and out into the cold night air.

Autumn had arrived, and with it, the frigid winds of the south sea.

Shivering, I hunched in my jacket, shifting closer to Trent.

"Couldn't resist me?" he asked, wrapping an arm around my shoulders.

"Something like that."

I wasn't the kind of person who could hide my emotions. Hell, I wasn't the kind of guy who lied successfully. Poker nights were a nightmare for me as my siblings and friends tended to swindle me out of the house and home.

Tee slowed, his steps dragging. "You okay?"

I nodded, swallowing the words that burned to be said.

I love you. I love you. I love you.

"So about throwing me over your shoulder...." I said lightly.

Tee chuckled, bumping me with his hip. "We'll see. Tomorrow will be just the—"

We both stilled as the thick scent of smoke carried along the breeze.

"People could be lighting their fireplaces early," I murmured, lifting my head.

Tee shook his head slowly, his lips thinning into a single line. "The wind is blowing across the bay. That's nothing out that way except the University and—"

"The resort. Damn."

I dropped my arm from around his waist, running a hand through my hair.

"I'll call it in." He pulled his mobile from his pants.

"Do it on the way," I ordered.

"We're going?"

I nodded. "If there's a kid there, we gotta make sure they're out and unhurt. The station's across town. At best, it'll take them another thirty to get to the resort. It'll only take us ten."

He swore softly. "I'll drive. You call."

I made the report as Tee raced us through the streets, weaving around sharp bends.

"We should have done more," I fretted, tapping my hands against my knee. "We should have tried harder to make contact."

"Don't," Trent said, reaching over to squeeze my knee. "We did what we thought was right."

The red glow guided us, the black smoke billowing towards us.

"Shit," I swore, catching sight of the resort as we crested the hill. "It's an inferno."

Flames licked the old timber, the greedy fire flicking embers high into the sky. Half the resort burned, the other barely visible through the thick smoke.

"Fuck."

Tee pulled the truck to a stop a fair distance from the flames. "This is bad."

I reached into his back seat, digging through the piles of clothing to tug two thick jackets free.

"Here," I tossed him one, kicking open the passenger door. "Cover your face with your shirt."

Trent exited the cab of his truck and headed to the tray at the back. Opening a metal, insulated storage container, he removed a small extinguisher, a fire blanket, two torches, and two small axes.

I raised an eyebrow.

He tossed me a flashlight and axe. "Hazard of the trade—always be prepared."

We approached the building from the rear, busting in a rickety door with a few sharp kicks.

"Five minutes," Trent ordered, leading the way. "Then we're back out. I'm not risking both our necks on a potential ghost."

Our torches guided the way, though the light barely cut through the thick, turbulent swirls.

"Is anyone here?" I yelled, trying not to breathe too deeply. "Hello?"

"I don't like this," Trent said, shaking his head as he opened another room, poking his head in. "This place is kindling."

We cleared the rear of the property, working our way down toward the fire. The smoke grew hotter, making it difficult to breathe. Heat radiated out toward us, embers flickered and caught on the wooden beams above us.

We rounded a corner and hit the inferno. The long hall was aflame, years of debris, old timber and a hot, dry summer encouraged the hungry blaze.

"We have to go!" Trent yelled, struggling to be heard over the roaring flames.

"I know, just one more—"

"Help!"

We both froze.

"Please!" the tiny, weak voice yelled, punctured by coughing. "Help!"

"Fuck!" Trent tossed me his flashlight and pulled out the tab of his extinguisher.

"Where are you?" I shouted, tucking the torch into my pants.

"Help!"

We made our way down the hall, kicking in doors and dodging falling chunks of wood and plaster.

"Clear," I yelled, kicking in a hotel door.

"Clear," Trent responded, doing the same on the opposite side.

We worked in tandem, smoke charring our lungs, and searing our throats.

"Clear," Trent called.

I kicked at a supply closet door. The lock didn't budge.

"In here!" the voice called. "Please! Help!"

"Found you! Stand back." I kicked at the door again, grunting when it didn't let go.

"Move," Trent barked, his voice raw. Tears streamed down my face, my lungs protesting each movement as I gasped for air.

He lifted a leg kicking once, twice, three times at the lock.

The fucking thing didn't move.

Grunting, Trent lifted his axe, heaving it into the door.

I picked up his discarded extinguisher as he hacked into the door frame, desperately spraying at the flames to keep those closest at bay.

It was like an ant taking on an elephant—a useless endeavour.

The frame finally gave way, and Trent shoved his way into the room.

The kid huddled in the far corner, his face pale, filthy, and tear-stained. A small backpack clutched in his arms. The room smelled faintly of chemicals and musty paper. There was a sleeping back shoved in one corner, and one of the bags we'd left for him in another.

"I'm sorry," the boy sobbed, coughing heavily. "I was cold and—"

"Is there anyone else here?" Trent asked, glancing around.

The boy shook his head.

"Come on." I offered him a hand. "We're getting out of here."

The kid made to stand but fell, coughing, his lips blue.

I dropped the now spent extinguisher as Trent ripped open the fire blanket and threw it around the child. Hauling the kid up into his arms and tossing him over his shoulder, he gave me a nod.

"Let's go."

Heart in my throat, I led the way back into the inferno.

In the few minutes it had taken for us to search for the boy, the fire had engulfed most of the rear of the building. Flames singed our hair and clothing. My skin felt as if it were being drawn tight and boiled, the heat seared the moisture from my pores.

Hunching, coughing, gasping, I hacked our way through to a hotel room. Crossing to a window, I used the axe to bust through the glass gasping as cool night air streamed into the smoke-filled room. Shrugging off my coat, I tossed it across the jagged edges of the window, and stepped outside, turning to accept the child from Trent.

He handed me the kid gently, our watery gazes meeting in relief.

I accepted the bundle, stepping back to allow him to exit. He picked up my discarded axe and followed me away from the blaze.

Coughing, gasping, and choking, we made it back to his truck as the crew arrived.

"Fuck," Teddy said, jumping down from the cab. "You guys look horrible."

I slumped down beside Trent's truck, leaning against it, the kid in my arms. "He's—he's—"

Coughs wracked my body.

"I got him." She dropped an emergency first aid kit beside me, tugging out an oxygen kit. "Here we go, slow breaths little dude. That's it."

The oxygen mask was fitted over the kid's filthy face, his eyes wide as his chest frantically moved, trying to draw breath.

Trent dropped beside me, wrapping an arm around my shoulders. He pressed a kiss to my temple, grimacing when ash came away.

"Never again," he swore, his voice raw.

I nodded, coughing.

Behind Teddy, the crew moved in a well-practised dance, rolling out hoses and establishing a perimeter.

"Anyone else in there?" she asked, rolling out her medical kit.

"Not that we saw," Tee said, turning away to cough.

Teddy tsked under her breath. "You know better than to run into a burning building without proper equipment and backup."

I bristled, feeling protective of Trent.

"If not for him—"

She flicked me a grin. "Calm your farm, Ryan. He's not in trouble, I'd have done the same thing." She winked at Trent. "But I am the boss and therefore need to chastise you."

"Consider me—" he coughed. "Duly chastised."

"What's your name, sweetie?" Teddy asked the kid.

He glanced up at me and I nodded reassuringly.

"Seth."

"Pleased to meet you, Seth." Teddy held up her hands and wiggled her fingers. "You okay if I check you over?"

He nodded and she took up his hand, checking his pulse.

The kid settled, beginning to breathe semi-normally. A second crew arrived a little while later along with police, an ambulance and a reporter.

I ignored all the action, my focus on Trent and the little boy in my arms.

Seth couldn't have been more than ten. Skinny, and scrawny with a mop of filthy reddish-brown hair and a weary distrustful look in his eyes.

My heart skipped, my stomach sinking.

He reminded me of me. Scared, alone, desperate.

He clung to Trent and me as the paramedics moved us into one of the ambulances to look us over. Trent made to step away but the kid reached out, his small fist clinging to Trent's shirt.

My heart fractured and I knew what I

needed to do.

This kid was coming home with me.

I met Trent's gaze over Seth's head.

"I'm good here," he said, settling back on the trolley beside me.

The ambulance crew gave us all a thorough once over then transported us to the hospital. My phone began to blow up before we'd even left the site.

DOGG PACK CHAT

MUMMYDOGG

RYAN! WHAT IS HAPPENING???
YOU WERE IN A FIRE????

DADDYDOGG

Son, this better be a joke.

MR.JAYKENTON

Dude, I know you're into
firefighters but seriously, did you
really need to run into a burning
building to get some action?

JAMESDOGG

Are you okay? What do you
need?

SAMDOGG

Is Trent with you? Has anyone
notified his family? I can walk
down and let Faye know.

HAYDENDOGG

Please tell me they've at least caught the menace who keeps setting things alight. This is getting out of hand.

ASHDOGG

We can see the fire from our place. Looks like an inferno. Do you want us to meet you at the hospital?

FRANKIEKENTON

Ryan, we're on the way to the hospital. Your brother might joke but he's beside himself.

MR.JAYKENTON

I am not.

FRANKIEKENTON

He is.

DADDYDOGG

We all are. We'll meet you at the hospital.

MUMMYDOGG

I'm bringing cookies and coffee. Sam, bringing a change of clothes for them. And yes, notify Faye. Can someone babysit Jeanene?

HAYDENDOGG

Kat has volunteered. She'll rally at your place.

ASHDOGG

We'll drop the kids off shortly. Millie will help.

FRANKIEKENTON

We'll bring some mattresses. The kids can have an impromptu sleepover.

MILLIEDOGG

I'll start baking. Ryan and Trent aren't going to want to think about cooking for a few days.

HAZELDOGG

Great point! I can help.

ENIDTENIL

Kat just called Henry. We're on our way. We can babysit.

HENRYTENIL

We'll hold down the kid fort while you guys head to the hospital.

KATDOGG

Thanks! We'll be there in about twenty.

I sighed, leaning into Trent as the ambulance bumped its way into town.

"What?" he asked, wrapping me and the sleeping Seth in his arms.

I handed him my phone.

He chuckled, scrolling through the messages. "And I thought my family was crazy."

"Don't even get me started."

He kissed my cheek. "Admit it. You love it."

I grinned. "It's where I belong."

Trent handed me back the cell. "Better respond or they'll go wild."

RYANDOGG

Hey all, Trent and I are okay. Not sure who blew the whistle on this but it sounds like they made it seem more dramatic than it was. Yes, we went into a burning building but we did it for a good cause. We're fine—a little dirty and a bit smoky but we're both good. Just going to the hospital for checks. We'll be home and ready for a shower and a nap before you know it.

I lifted the phone and snapped a picture of us, filthy but grinning and sent it off.

It only occurred to me later that this was our first picture since getting back together.

My phone exploded.

"Damn," I muttered, scrolling through the

messages. "Apparently, the picture didn't reassure them."

Seth shifted against my chest, muttering something in his sleep.

I adjusted, ignoring my protesting muscles.

Shoving the phone in my pocket, I leaned back against Trent, letting his heat warm my back.

"When you said you'd show me a good time, this isn't what I thought you meant," he said against my ear.

I grinned, tilting my head back to look up at him. "What? You didn't expect sparks?"

He grinned, the movement cracking the layers of ash on his face. "Alas, no. Not literal ones anyway."

I turned away, coughing a little. Trent's hand smoothed across my back, holding me steady.

I settled back against him, surprised the kid hadn't woken up.

"What are we gonna do about this?" he asked, cupping Seth's head gently.

I swallowed, already knowing there was only one option. "Once Child Protective Services concludes their investigation, he'll either be reunited with his family or placed with a foster family."

Trent's arms flinched around me. "He'll go into the system?"

I nodded. "It's how this works."

He was quiet for a moment. "But you don't want that?"

I hesitated. "No. It feels like we should give the kid a fighting chance."

"We?"

I blanched, pulling away from him. "Shit, I meant—"

His finger pressed against my lips. "I agree."

I stilled.

Tee gently cupped my face. "Tonight was intense and I don't want to add to your emotional toll but, Ryan, I love you. I've always loved you. I'm sorry for being an ass and not recognising what a treasure you are ten years ago. I'm sorry that it took me longer to work out who I am and what I want. But let me be clear, those questions have been answered. I want you. I want us. I want what you said—the growing together and choosing each other until it becomes so ingrained that there is no other choice. I want that for us. And—" he nodded at the precious cargo in my arms. "If he's part of the deal as well, so much the better. I got a lot of love to give, Ry. And I want to walk through this life loving you, loving those you love, and basking in your love."

I sucked in a breath. "Are you asking me to marry you?"

He grinned. "Not just yet. When I propose, it's gonna be the best-goddamned proposal you've ever had."

That emotion to which I'd never aspired burst through me—joy. Pure and simple, beautiful and unique.

"I love you too," I whispered.

He brushed a thumb across my cheek. "I know."

We kissed—not in the way of passion, but in the way of promise. A gentle meeting of souls who were committing to each other for infinite time.

EPILOGUE 1

Ryan

Two years later

Seth twitched at the bowtie around his neck, tugging at it viciously.

"You can take it off if you want," I reminded him.

He shook his head stubbornly, dropping his hand.

I hid a smile. "Seriously, dude. It's okay."

His bottom lip pushed out—a sure sign that I'd triggered his mulishness.

"I want to wear it."

I struggled to keep a straight face. "Alright. But just know that as soon as the pictures are done, I'm ripping mine off."

His quicksilver grin flashed, and I couldn't help but ruffle his hair.

He shoved me away with a laugh. "Dad!"

My heart swelled, and yet again, I questioned how it was possible to contain so much love and joy.

My dad cleared his throat, and I straightened, turning to watch the end of the aisle.

There he stood, locked arm in arm with his parents—my soon-to-be husband.

How did I get so lucky?

He'd made good on his promise—the proposal had come as a surprise and a delight. Filled with whimsy and laughter, he'd laid a treasure map out for Seth and me to follow. Clues led to different locations around the Cove until we ended up back on the beach where we'd all first met.

The resort had been dismantled; the charred ruins carted away until all that remained was a cracked, concrete block. The location stood vacant, with only a single for sale sign planted along the road.

It was there that Trent crouched, on one knee, holding a ring.

And it was there that he'd asked Seth's permission to marry me.

Everything had moved quickly after the fire. Trent had moved in, and we'd petitioned the court to become Seth's temporary guardians while an investigation was conducted.

The kid had run from foster homes, and been living rough for a few weeks. He'd lit the fires because he'd been cold and desperate. But the poor guy had been exhausted—and each fire had been caused because he'd fallen asleep.

Proposing there had been perfect—after all, it was there that we'd found each other and become a family.

I pulled Seth in for a quick hug.

"Dad," he complained, pushing at me. "Stop with the mushy."

I laughed, letting him go. "Okay, okay. I'll stop."

Sam's band started playing a version of *Blossom* by Dermot Kennedy, the words adjusted slightly but still ringing true.

Our life was like a dream I never wanted to forget. This man, he held my heart. He'd always held my heart.

Trent walked slowly down the aisle, past friends and family dressed in an explosion of colour. Past reams of flowers, and past bubbles being blown by the cacophony of kidlets that were squirming in their finery.

Unshed tears formed a lump, clogging my throat as his gaze met mine, his smile wide, gorgeous, and filled with joy.

"Love you," he mouthed as he walked toward me.

I grasped desperately for control, struggling not to break down. Seth brought about my failure.

He leaned against me and whispered just loud enough to be heard over the music.

"We're a family."

A sob broke free, tears flowing down my cheeks as Trent drew close. He reached for me as I reached for him. Hugging tight, our foreheads pressed together, we laughed, basking in the love of today.

"I choose you. I choose us," he whispered, gently brushing a kiss across my lips. "Again, and again until it is no choice at all."

"You were never a choice," I admitted. "It's always been you."

We separated only to step under the flower arbour, our hands joined together as we pledged our life and love.

Today and forever.

EPILOGUE 2

Trent

A year later

Sun filtered through a gap in the curtains, bathing the room in a hint of cool winter light.

I automatically listened for the kids but knew without moving that they were still in bed, sleeping away last night's excess.

We'd allowed them to stay up far past midnight as they'd raced around the backyard with their cousins, begging to stay up just a little longer, a little longer, a little longer.

Lips caressed my shoulder, a hand grazing along my hip. My body woke under his hands, desire flaring like a small spark into a delicious crackling fire.

"Morning," Ryan murmured as he continued his gentle caress. "Happy New Year."

I sighed, closing my eyes and relaxing back against him. "Mm. Any resolutions this year?"

"Just one." The blankets lifted as he shimmied down the bed.

He took me in his mouth, his tongue lashing my crown.

"Fuck," I groaned, arching my hips. "Babe, what are you—"

"Enacting my resolution," he said.

"And that is?" I asked but he didn't respond; his mouth closed over my swollen tip and he sucked deep.

My breath rushed out on a quiet curse.

Ryan worked me, his filthy mouth worshipping my dick.

"Fuck," I grunted, pushing my hips up to get my dick deeper into his throat. "Make me come."

He pulled away from my dick with a pop. "No."

"No?" I growled, reaching for him.

He shifted on the bed, moving away from my hand.

"No. I want you in me."

Already drugged with need, I hauled him in for a hot kiss before shoving him off me.

"On your back, put those knees in the air."

I pulled the lube from our bedside table as he positioned himself on the bed, his gaze locked with mine.

Fuck, he's gorgeous.

This man, my husband, my partner, my one choice in life—he constantly surprised and delighted me.

And right now, he turned me the fuck on.

I am a very lucky man.

I moved behind him, running one hand over his ass as I stroked lube down my shaft.

"You going to stand there and watch all day or do something?" Ryan protested, shifting restlessly. He watched my hand slide lazily up and down my cock, his face flushing, his eyes growing feverishly hot.

That's it, baby. Watch me.

"Just admiring the view." I nudged his legs further apart, grinning at his low, appreciative huff.

My man didn't mind being dominated once in a while.

I ran my cock along his ass, grinning when his head tipped back. I lube him up slowly, teasing him until Ryan is a flexing, vibrating mess of need.

"You want this, baby?" I asked, jerking my dick roughly.

"Fuck yes."

I rubbed the head of my cock against him and gently, slowly, push in, savouring his muttered curse. He wanted more, but I relished teasing him and drawing out our pleasure.

Ryan's legs wrapped around me, and I snaked a hand between us to fist his cock. His ass may be my favourite place in the world, but his cock was a close second.

"You ready?" I asked, my voice rough.

"Fuck me."

I pounded into him with deep, desperate, rough thrusts. His cock is leaking against my belly, easing the slide of my hand along his dick.

While I'm loving every second of this wild ride—I know exactly how to make it even better.

I shifted, adjusting my angle until I hit his prostate with each thrust.

And just like that, Ryan lost the power of speech.

I leaned down, catching his mouth in a sweaty, delicious kiss. I fucked his ass, thrusting harder and harder, desperate to push him over the edge before I lost all control.

"Fuck, Tee, I'm gonna—"

His hot cum spurted onto my abs, and I

could no longer withhold my release. I fucked into him and groaned as my orgasm ripped through me, leaving me a shaking, unsettled mess on my husband's chest.

Ryan wrapped his arms around me, holding me tight as we both fought to catch our breath.

"That's one resolution down," he murmured, snuggling into my shoulder.

"You have more?"

"I have a whole lifetime."

Grinning, I kissed him and tasted the promise on his lips.

My phone buzzed just as Ryan's did as well.

We exchanged a glance.

"What new hell is about to hit us?" he murmured reaching for his cell.

With a quick swipe, I watched as his eyebrows rose, his lips parting in surprise.

"What?" I asked, sitting up.

"Your.... My.. our...." Words seemed to fail him. "Shit."

He handed me the phone. Texts were coming fast and furious in the family group chat as I read the article one of his siblings had linked.

"Your brother has married my sister," I said, unable to believe what I was reading. "When the hell did Faye and Sam start dating?"

Ryan shook his head mutely.

"Well." I tossed his phone onto the bedside table. "Welcome to the family I guess."

He spluttered, his mouth moving in a silent laugh. "Trent!"

I grinned, pulling him back down into my arms. "I think our relationship might be considered illegal now?"

"TRENT!"

Chuckling, I nuzzled kisses into his neck. "Happy New Year, baby."

He sighed, holding me tight. "Love you. Even if you're terrible."

"Love you too. Always."

My dearest greedy readers, thank you so much for reading Trent and Ryan's story. If you'd like a little more of them check out the bonus extra on my website
EvieMitchell.com

ABOUT THE AUTHOR

Evie Mitchell is a thirty-something romance author (she/her/hers) living with disability. She believes in inclusion, accessibility, and fierce romance. Her loves include steamy romance novels, her husband, their THREE sausage dogs (heaven help her), and her ever-growing collection of book-related mugs.

As a woman with a diverse work history including in areas such as emergency response, event management, human rights, disability access, and security - her books are filled with true stories (bridezillas), worst-case scenarios (malfunctioning dresses), and her favorite tropes (one-bed).

Evie specialises in fiercely inclusive happily ever afters.

www.EvieMitchell.com

ALSO BY EVIE MITCHELL

Capricorn Cove Series

The Shake-Up

Double the D

Muffin Top

The Mrs. Clause

New Year Knew You

Double Breasted

As You Wish

You Sleigh Me

Resolution Revolution

Meat Load

Larsson Siblings Series

Thunder Thighs

Clean Sweep

The X-list

Reality Check

The Christmas Contract

Dogg Pack Books

Puppy Love

Bad English
The Frock Up
Pier Pressure
Trick or Trent

All Access Series
Knot My Type
Love Flushed

Nameless Souls MC Series
Runner
Wrath
Ghost
Shield

Elliot Security Series
Rough Edge
Bleeding Edge